Dear Lavinia,

We are finally in Oregon, the cabin is built, and I can write you a letter. You know with what doubts I left our old farm in Kentucky, and how it hurt my heart to leave my dear mother and father. I would not let my husband, Will, pan for gold, but I did agree that free land was too good an opportunity to miss.

    As I write on my lap desk, my three older ones—Amanda, Lonnie, and Caleb—sit at the table, writing in their journals. They kept them all the way west to remind them of our adventures. They look on the whole trip as a lark, but I cannot forget the many graves I saw along the wagon trail. Cholera took so many from families going west to find gold. But God protected us and we came through.

    Maybe someday a descendant of ours will find these journals and read of the trials and hopes of three young people. And maybe they will find the picture taken of us soon after our daughter Columbia was born. We look tired but full of hope. Dear friend, write soon. I miss you.

                           Your loving friend,
                           Grace

Mississippi Mud

THREE PRAIRIE JOURNALS

by Ann Turner ~ pictures by Robert J. Blake

HARPERCOLLINSPUBLISHERS

Amanda

Leaving

When our wagon was packed
and waiting in the drive,
I saw it as a stranger would:
Pa in front, stiff as a portrait,
Ma beside, fidgeting her skirt,
and Gran and Grandpa gripping the porch rail
as if they could not stand.

Caleb, Lonnie, Nell, and me sat in back
looking out the puckered hole,
and I thought our wishes rose
to the sky like smoke.

I wanted to ride a horse astride,
let the wind whip my hair loose,
run skinny-legged down prairie slopes,
and shout out the holler
that was always in my throat.

Caleb wanted marbles, twelve of them,
with a blue agate for shooting,
storms that brought cool air,
and a horse with a black mane.

Nell was too young for wishes,
and Lonnie's a farmer. I knew
he wanted a peach orchard,
and earth that was deep and rich.

So much we wanted,
none of it came the way we thought:
storms, wind, a horse with a black mane,
a baby with a pink face,
and land where I could run and shout
with no one to tell me
I was not a lady.

Used Up

The land was used up,
thin as muslin,
and the trees by our creek drooped
over water black
where catfish died.
Even Grandpa's peaches
tasted bitter and mealy.
I was glad to leave.
Pa whistled high,
the oxen swung their horns,
Caleb cheered, and suddenly
my eyes squeezed shut on Gran
standing on the porch,
on Grandpa waving his red bandana
like a flag.

Driving

Pull hard on the left rein,
shout, "Haw!" and their heads do go
where you want.
Pull hard on the right, shout, "Gee!"
and watch out for ravines and gulleys.
Keep the wheels off the rocky shoulder
of the road,
if there is a road.
And if the oxen scare,
eyes rolling, horns tossing,
why, just hold on
and hope you don't die.

I'm not afraid. If I can cook
under an umbrella, wash clothes
in the swift rivers, and make sure
Nell don't fall under the wagon wheels,
I guess I can drive an old team of oxen.

Love

When we stopped by the Platte,
the wagons gathered together
like ladies at a sewing circle,
talk flew up from the fires,
kids ran and hollered,
and boys shot stones into the dark.
Melinda, a girl like an eager chicken,
and Cassie, her skinny sister,
sat with me and talked of love.
They thought it had a face:
sharp, mustached, handsome,
with words ready to pull you in
so sweet, no way to say no.
I was quiet. Canvas flapped,
a fiddle tuned up,
notes plucking at the stars.
The warm dark settled like a blanket,
and I thought *this* is love, this
is the best there is.

Town

I waited all day for stores,
people laughing, candy,
for some calico cloth blue
as prairie flowers in the grass.

It's gone already, like a peppermint sliver
swallowed up whole.
Two dogs (one yellow),
three men in overalls
shouting about the weather,
two ladies in faded pink
like mosquito netting,
and a child with a smeary nose.

Ma says we will make our own town.
I sit in the wagon,
looking out at grass and sky and wonder:
What if ours is no better?
What if after all this way
what we come to is less
than what we left behind?

Someday Someone

We heard the tale in town,
how the first settlers come spring
found the ox-hide tent
with dirt piled up the sides,
a trickle of smoke above.
She came out foot first,
like a babe born the wrong way:
a thin arm, one shoulder, dress torn,
then her head all full of lice,
tangles, and bits of skin.

The settlers sat in their wagons, afraid,
till she said, "My name is Mary,"
her voice creaky as an old swing.
"They all died last fall."
She stopped and leaned against the wagon.
The words poured out, her mouth
an open wound, how Ma and Pa
and five brothers were killed from behind,
and only she, hiding in the pine brush,
escaped.

"How did you live?" the settlers asked.
"I skinned the oxen, dried the meat,
got brush for fire. I knew"—
she stopped for breath—
"someday someone would come."

Astride

No one saw me creep
out of the cabin,
the sky pink as our baby's face.
I borrowed Caleb's horse,
gentled enough to let me swing
up and hold the rope.
Off we went, across
the stumpy field, as my legs
gripped the horse tight.
I opened my mouth
and hollered so loud and long,
I woke the geese in the yard,
and they shouted back.

Caleb

Good-bye

Say good-bye
to cornfields by the river,
to Grandpa's barn where I
smoked tobacco and got sick,
to the catfish river Luke, Jim, and me
swam in, and the old trout hid.
Say good-bye to Gran's pies
cooling on the window sill,
to Grandpa's mustache
tickling me good night.

"Hold on tight!" Pa shouts.
The cat hides in Nell's lap,
the road turns, the farmhouse slips
out of sight like a fish off a hook
and I blow my nose,
good-bye.

Good Luck Charms

Luke says you got to have
one for river crossings,
for the woods at night,
for the wild men waiting to rob
the wagon, tie up your ma,
and steal the horses.

I was so fired with fear
by the time I left,
I looked like a peddler
selling wares, all hung
around my neck—
rabbit's foot for water,
snakeskin for woods,
and a dead man's fingernail
to keep off the horse-stealing,
ma-hurting wild men.

Alfred

That cat Alfred
made a place in the wagon
when we left Kentucky,
curled beside the bean sack
like he owned it.

Ma kept trying to move him.
"Come, Alfred, here kitty!"
He'd have none of it—
paws set, ears pricked,
he knew all he had to do was sit.

Even after the rough crossings,
when water came up
the wagon sides
and soaked our bedding,
and he climbed the bean sack
to get dry,
he didn't leave the wagon
till Pa built a cabin bed
he could sleep on.

Sweet Pipe

People pack the strangest things,
then leave them once the way gets rough.
I saw a cradle by the road,
a grandpa clock still ticking,
a desk all carved with vines and flowers.
We took just the necessaries:
dried meat, beans and flour,
and a gold coin sewn up
in Pa's vest pocket.
Lonnie brought peach seeds,
Amanda her diary, and Nell a rag doll.
I carried my pennywhistle west,
that high sound piping
out of the wagon back,
up to the black sky
and the so many stars, I thought
they might fall down
to say hello.

Jake

Pa says it's no use mourning a dog,
but he don't sleep regular
now Jake is gone. He followed us
all the way west from Kentucky,
trotting in the shade of the wagon.
Once Nell sat playing
and a snake coiled by her foot.
Jake barked and nipped till
that snake whipped out of sight.

I can't stand how he just wore out;
he didn't twitch, breathe,
or lick my face one day.
We dug a grave, piled rocks on top.
I can't help crying when I think
how he'd hate those rocks
and the coyotes walking over him.

Horse

I never could abide cruelty to an animal,
and when I saw that man whip his horse
till the flank showed red,
I jumped off the wagon,
no use Ma's hand on my sleeve.
I grabbed the halter
and soothed that frightened horse.
Pa asked, "How much you want?"
Man rubbed his nose, spat, said,
"Ten dollars," which we can't lose,
but Pa slapped that money on his hand
and never looked behind.
I put goose grease on the horse's flank,
walked him slow, called him Jake.
Pa says I'll ride Jake soon,
soon I'll feel that black mane in my face,
his four legs carrying me home.

Mississippi Mud

The wheels were caked
with Mississippi mud.
The inside hub of the wheel
kept its patch even after thunder
sent the oxen running
into the river, and Pa had to catch them
with the last of the corn Ma was
fixing to make pancakes with.
That mud stayed after a windstorm
stopped us on the prairie,
tail end to the gale, and Ma prayed,
her face like a white handkerchief.
One night the last of the mud fell
into my hand; I saved it in a pouch.
I'll bury it under my bed for luck,
for the sticking strength
of the Mississippi mud.

Lonnie

Lonnie's Wish

Pa was so restless, Ma said
he'd wear a path from door to town.
"Peaches big as babies' heads!
Cool, sweet summers," he shouted.
Ma bit her lip and was silent.
So we went,
the wagon packed and snug,
Ma in her big red apron
(did she think we didn't know?),
Jake trotting by the wheel.
The uncles sipped corn whiskey,
  the aunts jabbed handkerchiefs to their eyes,
  and Gran's mouth looked sewn shut.
    I wanted sky overhead
        with rain clouds fat and dark,
          soil deep as a man is tall,
          and a house with light shining out
            on a peach orchard, swaying in the wind.

Columbia

They never tell you,
not the important things.
But I'd been watching Ma's aprons,
how they got higher and higher.
I knew what was growing underneath.

At night I whispered to the apron child,
so soft no one could hear,
"When we get west,
I'll make you a cornhusk doll,
find Indian beads for a sky blue
necklace, and quail feathers for a hat."

Come the Columbia River,
Ma got her pains. Sweat on her face,
hands clenched, she said,
"Clem, it's time. Stop!"
Down Pa went, tethered the horses,
Ma moaned, "No woman near,
you'll have to help."

Pa stayed inside the wagon all day,
while we looked for buffalo chips
to fire the kettle.
We could hear Ma's cries,
like birds being killed in the sky.

When the stars pricked out
and owls called by the river,
Pa shouted to us,
"A sister—we'll call her Columbia.
Come see your ma."

Inside the wagon,
Ma looked white and leftover.
On her chest was a red scrap
that mewled and howled
just like a cat.
I held her up to the open back,
and said, "Look, Columbia, stars,
don't cry."

Seeds

When the dust gets in my mouth
I remember the taste of pork
roasted over hickory wood
the night before we left
and how Gran filled a sack
with peach pits,
like dried brown hearts to carry west.
Someday I'll dig some black sweet soil,
set each seed to catch the light,
and one day I'll watch those peaches ripen.
Each bite
will be a taste of our old farm.

Scare

We woke to sun on canvas
and the sky just beginning
through the wagon hole.
I heard Nell cry out,
her face crumpled yellow
as a buttercup left out in the cold.
Ma said, "Out! And don't come back
till I say!" Caleb touched his charm,
Amanda hung on to my shirt.
We sat by the creek, the wagon behind
like gunpowder about to go off
if I didn't watch it so.

Caleb and I fished, Amanda
piled rocks to a tower, and then
the tears ran down. She saw
the stones were like a grave.
Later, the owls moaned overhead,
fish slapped the dark water,
and I saw the wagon lurch and shake.

Pa called, his voice thick and loud,
"Nell's all right, come back."
We ran to the wagon;
none of us dared touch Nell
so small on the pillow.
Pa coughed, "It wasn't"—
he could not say the word—"cholera."
A bird whistled in the night sky,
Nell began to cry; it was then
Ma finally smiled.

Riders

The grass whistled in the wind,
clouds scattered overhead, and I
leaped on Pa's mare to ride away
from the wagon bunched with
beds, barrels, sacks,
to where grass met the sky.

I galloped toward that place,
but it kept running ahead.
Sudden hoofbeats thudded by my ear,
and I saw a boy-horse thundering beside.
It took my heart
to see his dark hair streaming,
skin rippling,
eyes bright as the black creek.
I hated how he knew that earth,
while I was just a rider
jolting on a horse,
looking for home.

Picture

Smack in the dusty middle
of town, a wagon was stopped,
a man in front with a black box.
"Pictures!" Ma cried.
"To keep forever. Quick!"
She fussed our hair, twitched our clothes,
wet Pa's beard, wild as a thistle.
"Don't move!" the man shouted.
Nell began to wail,
Caleb and Amanda fidgeted,
and Columbia waved her fists.
My smile got lost
in my shirt collar.

We're fixed forever in that frame:
Pa stiff as a preacher,
the baby hiding Ma's face,
the rest all blurred from restless moving.
But I am that solemn, eager stranger
I might like to meet someday.

Home

The wagon's unpacked,
finally,
the cabin built from forest logs,
curtains sewn from the sheet
Caleb tore in a bad dream
after Jake died.
Garden'll have to wait till spring.
The well is filled with water sweet,
the beds are still at night.
Columbia sleeps snug in her cradle,
Nell curls against Amanda's back.
At night I stand in the door,
looking out over our new land.
Soon the forest will come down.
Soon we'll start the orchard.
But now the pegged door swings wide
and makes a path of light
for us to walk on.

For Karen Schweitzer,

who loves journeys

—A.T.

For my uncle, Edward Duffy

—R.B.

Mississippi Mud: Three Prairie Journals Text copyright © 1997 by Ann Turner   Illustrations copyright © 1997 by Robert J.
Blake   Printed in the U.S.A. All rights reserved. Library of Congress Cataloging-in-Publication Data Turner, Ann Warren.
Mississippi mud : three prairie journals / by Ann Turner ; pictures by Robert J. Blake.   p.   cm.   Summary: Poems
reflecting the points of view of three pioneer children describe their family's journey from Kentucky to Oregon.   ISBN 0-
06-024432-1 — ISBN 0-06-024433-X (lib. bdg.)   1. Frontier and pioneer life—West (U.S.)—Juvenile poetry.   2. Voyages
and travels—Juvenile poetry.   3. Family—West (U.S.)—Juvenile poetry.   4. Children's poetry, American.   [1. Frontier
and pioneer life—West (U.S.)—Poetry.   2. Overland journeys to the Pacific—Poetry.   3. Family life—West (U.S.)—Poetry.
4. American poetry.]   I. Blake, Robert J., ill. II. Title. PS3570.U665M57 1997 95-10850 811'.54—dc20   CIP   AC
Typography by Al Cetta   1 2 3 4 5 6 7 8 9   10 ❖   First Edition